BOYOGI

How a Wounded Family Learned to Heal

David Barclay Moore

illustrated by Noa Denmon

CANDLEWICK PRESS

A WHILE AGO, my daddy came home from far away.

But he came home different than before he left.

Before he left, Daddy used to sleep like a log. And he liked to talk a lot.

After he came home, Daddy had nightmares, and he spent a lot of time alone.

Before, he was fun to be around. We used to run races in the park.

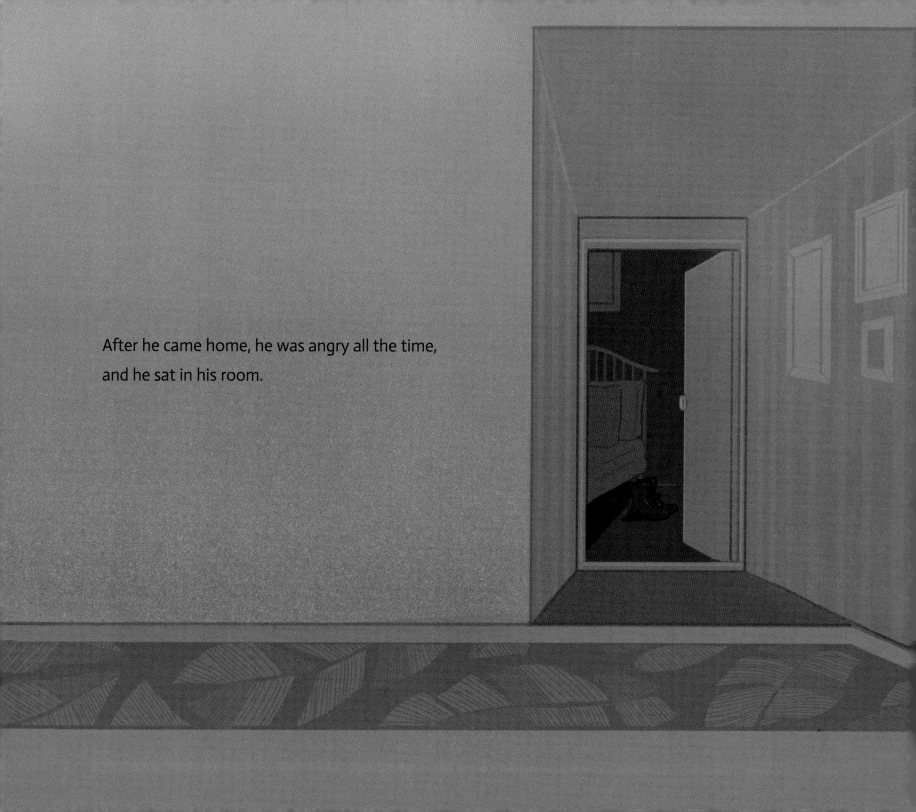

After he came home, he was angry all the time,
and he sat in his room.

After Daddy came home, I thought he acted sad because of something I did. I thought my daddy didn't love me anymore.

Mama said, "Of course your father loves you, Butta Bean. It's just that Daddy got sick overseas. That has nothing to do with you. He needs time to get better."

"Where is Daddy sick?" I asked. "Is it his tummy?"

"No," said Mama.

"Is it his knee?" I asked. Last summer, I skinned my knee and that hurt a lot.

"No," said Mama. "It's not Daddy's knee that hurts him."

"Is it his head?" I asked Mama. "Does Daddy's head hurt?"

Mama was quiet for a minute, and then she smiled at me. "Well, yes, Butta Bean. It *is* his head. When Daddy was away, some bad things happened there. And those things made him sick. We are lucky nothing happened to Daddy's *body.* But those bad things harmed his *mind.*"

I didn't know what she meant.

Mama asked me, "Do you know what your mind is?"

I shook my head.

She touched my forehead. "Your mind is in here. It's the things you think about. It's how you feel happy or sad. It's the songs you like to sing and your favorite colors. Our minds are very precious, and we need to take care of them. Your mind is what makes you *you*. Daddy's is what makes Daddy *Daddy*."

I thought I understood then.

"Mama?" I said.

"Yes, Baby?"

"When my tummy hurts, you give me peppermint tea and honey to help me feel better. When I skin my knee, you stick a Band-Aid on it."

"Yes. That's right."

"How do we make Daddy's head better?"

Mama thought for a long time. "Butta Bean, that's what we're trying to figure out," she said finally.

The next week, Mama took Daddy and me with her to the YMCA a
few blocks from our apartment. The YMCA was where Mama went to
exercise and take dance classes.

Daddy didn't want to go, but Mama wouldn't let up until he put on
his coat and walked with us.

The Y was full of grown-ups working out and sweating. Downstairs in the basement, Mama and Daddy changed clothes and took a class called yoga. I sat on the floor in the corner and watched.

As the class began, the instructor pressed his hands together and bowed.

"Namaste!" he said. "*Namaste* is from the old Sanskrit language. It means 'I bow to the spiritual within you.' I ask that you all please enter our space in a calm way. No angry thoughts. Speak softly. Positive thinking. I want you to move peacefully while you're here."

At first I thought yoga was weird. But it looked fun, like stretching but more cool. Most of the poses they did were standing, balancing, or bending in funny ways.

Daddy seemed to like it.

He liked it so much, he went back to yoga class the next day. Mama and I went with him again. This time I tried yoga, and I liked it, too. It made me feel like I had superpowers. Like I could do anything.

That day our teacher told us a *yogi* was anybody who did yoga.

Week after week, Daddy and I went to our yoga class in the basement of our YMCA, even after Mama stopped going with us. Daddy and I went whether it snowed or rained. Whether it was cloudy or sunny.

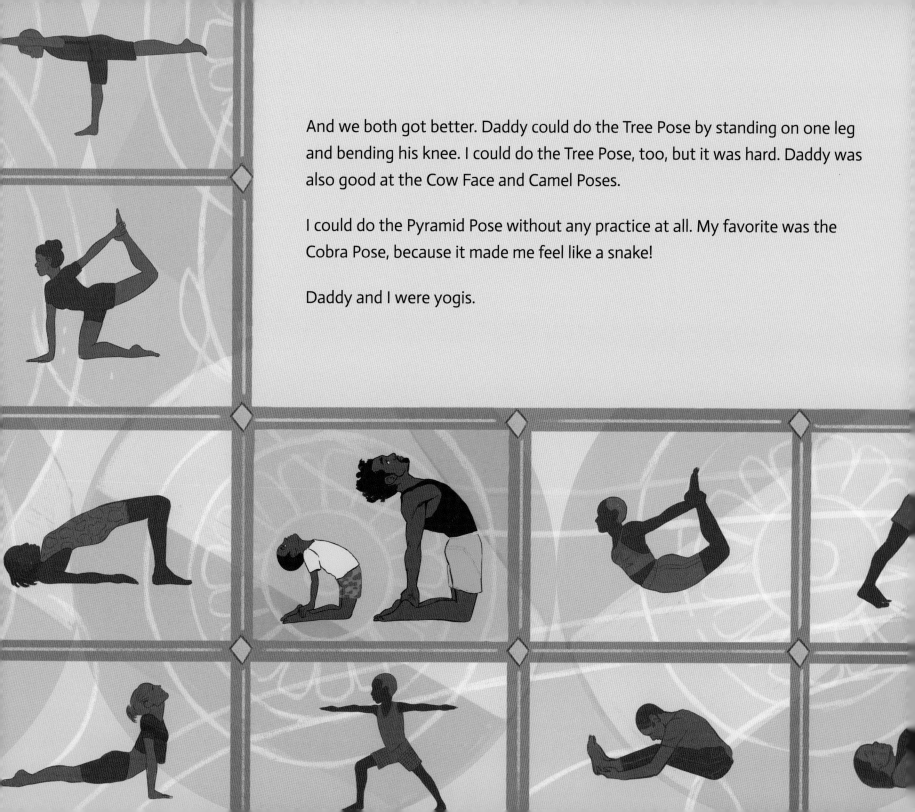

And we both got better. Daddy could do the Tree Pose by standing on one leg and bending his knee. I could do the Tree Pose, too, but it was hard. Daddy was also good at the Cow Face and Camel Poses.

I could do the Pyramid Pose without any practice at all. My favorite was the Cobra Pose, because it made me feel like a snake!

Daddy and I were yogis.

We walked home after class one day, and Daddy told me, "Butta Bean, boy, you're sure good at your poses!"

I felt proud.

"You're a regular little *boyogi*," Daddy said. We both laughed at how funny that word sounded. Daddy went on, "This yoga's helped me feel *way* better. I'm not as nervous as I was right after I came home from overseas. Not as jumpy and not as sad all the time. My therapist tells me yoga's helped a lot."

"I feel better, too," I said. "I used to feel sad because you got sad."

Daddy looked at me and grinned. I grinned back.

After that, he raced me home. Just like we used to do before.
As usual, I won. I always knew I could get ahead of Daddy.

Because he'll always love me, and I'll always love him.

In loving memory of all those special times I enjoyed with my own father,
John Nathaniel Moore Sr.—a steadfast, dedicated man and army veteran
DBM

To anyone finding a new beginning
ND

First edition 2023

Library of Congress Catalog Card Number 2022936607
ISBN 978-1-5362-1370-6

23 24 25 26 27 28 CCP 10 9 8 7 6 5 4 3 2 1

Printed in Shenzhen, Guangdong, China

This book was typeset in Actor.
The illustrations were created digitally.

Candlewick Press
99 Dover Street
Somerville, Massachusetts 02144

www.candlewick.com